CYBER QUEST

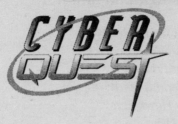

Books by Sigmund Brouwer

Lightning on Ice Series
#1 *Rebel Glory*
#2 *All-Star Pride*
#3 *Thunderbird Spirit*
#4 *Winter Hawk Star*
#5 *Blazer Drive*
#6 *Chief Honor*

Short Cuts Series
#1 *Snowboarding to the Extreme . . . Rippin'*
#2 *Mountain Biking to the Extreme . . . Cliff Dive*
#3 *Skydiving to the Extreme . . . 'Chute Roll*
#4 *Scuba Diving to the Extreme . . . Off the Wall*

CyberQuest Series
#1 *Pharaoh's Tomb*
#2 *Knight's Honor*
#3 *Pirate's Cross*
#4 *Outlaw's Gold* (available 10/97)

The Accidental Detectives Mystery Series

Winds of Light Medieval Adventures

Adult Books
Double Helix
Blood Ties

QUEST 3
PIRATE'S CROSS

SIGMUND BROUWER

NELSON™

Thomas Nelson, Inc.
Nashville

Pirate's Cross
Quest 3 in the *CyberQuest* Series

Copyright © 1997
by Sigmund Brouwer

Published in Nashville, Tennessee,
by Tommy Nelson™, a division of Thomas Nelson, Inc.

Managing Editor: Laura Minchew
Project Editor: Beverly Phillips
Cover illustration: Kevin Burke

Library of Congress Cataloging-in-Publication Data

Brouwer, Sigmund, 1959–
    Pirate's cross / Sigmund Brouwer.
        p. cm. — (CyberQuest ; #3)
    Summary: Mok's virtual reality adventures continue as the
twenty-first century Welfaro finds himself on board a pirate ship,
with a renegade pirate challenging his faith in God.
    ISBN 0-8499-4036-2
    [1. Science fiction.   2. Virtual reality—Fiction.
3. Pirates—Fiction   4. Christian life—Fiction.]   I. Title.
II. Series: Brouwer, Sigmund, 1959–   CyberQuest ; #3.
PZ7.B79984Pi   1997
[Fic]—dc21   97-17353
                                                          CIP
                                                          AC

Printed in the United States of America
97 98 99 00 01 02 OPM 9 8 7 6 5 4 3 2 1

**To the *Breakaway* readers
who added a lot of fun to the series**

CYBERQUEST SERIES TERMS

BODYWRAP — a sheet of cloth that serves as clothing.

THE COMMITTEE — a group of people dedicated to making the world a better place.

MAINSIDE — any part of North America other than Old Newyork.

MINI-VIDCAM — a hidden video camera.

NETPHONE — a public telephone with a computer keypad. For a minimum charge, users can send e-mail through the Internet.

OLD NEWYORK — the bombed out island of Manhattan transformed into a colony for convicts and the poorest of the poor.

TECHNOCRAT — an upper class person who can read, operate computers, and make much more money than a Welfaro.

'TRIC SHOOTER — an electric gun that fires enough voltage to stun its target.

VIDTRANS — video transmitters.

VIDWATCH — a watch with a mini television screen.

WATERMAN — a person who sells pure water.

WELFARO — a person living in the slums in Old Newyork.

THE GREAT WATER WARS—A.D. 2031. *In the year A.D. 2031 came the great Water Wars. The world's population had tripled during the previous thirty years. Worldwide demand for fresh, unpolluted water grew so strong that countries fought for control of water supplies. The war was longer and worse than any of the previous world wars. When it ended, there was a new world government, called the World United. The government was set up to distribute water among the world countries and to prevent any future wars. But it took its control too far.*

World United began to see itself as all important. After all, it had complete control of the world's limited water supplies. It began to make choices about who was "worthy" to receive water.

Very few people dared to object when World United denied water to criminals, the poor, and others it saw as undesirable. People were afraid of losing their own water if they spoke up.

One group, however, saw that the government's actions were wrong. These people dared to speak—Christians. They knew that only God should have control of their lives. They knew that they needed to stand up to the government for those who could not. Because of this, the government began to persecute the Christians and outlawed the Christian church. Some people gave up their beliefs to continue to receive an allotment of government water. Others refused and either joined underground churches or became hunted rebels, getting their water on the black market.

In North America, only one place was safe for the rebel Christians. The island of Old Newyork. The bombings of the great Water Wars had destroyed much of it, and the government used the entire island as a prison. The government did not care who else fled to the slums of those ancient street canyons.

Old Newyork grew in population. While most newcomers were criminals, some were these rebel Christians. Desperate for freedom, they entered this lion's den of lawlessness.

Limited water and supplies were sent from Mainside to Old Newyork, but some on Mainside said that any was too much to waste on the slums. When the issue came up at a World Senate meeting in 2049, it was decided that Old Newyork must be treated like a small country. It would have to provide something to the world in return for water and food.

When this new law went into effect, two things happened in the economy of this giant slum. First, work gangs began stripping steel from the skyscrapers. Anti-pollution laws on Mainside made it expensive to manufacture new steel. Old steel, then, was traded for food and water.

Second, when a certain Mainside business genius got caught evading taxes in 2053, he was sent to Old Newyork. There he quickly saw a new business opportunity—slave labor.

Old Newyork was run by criminals and had no laws. Who was there to stop him from forcing people to work for him?

Within a couple of years, the giant slum was filled with bosses who made men, women, and children work at almost no pay. They produced clothing on giant sewing machines and assembled cheap computer products. Even boys and girls as young as ten years old worked up to twelve hours a day.

Christians in Old Newyork, of course, fought against this. But it was a battle the Christians lost over the years. Criminals and factory bosses used ruthless violence to control the slums.

Christianity was forced to become an underground movement in the slums. Education, too, disappeared. As did any medical care.

Into this world, Mok was born.

PROLOGUE

OLD NEWYORK—A.D. 2076. Benjamin Rufus, a tired, old man, walked through the slums of Old Newyork for two hours before reaching the street corner of his memories.

By then, the sweat on his forehead felt as heavy and thick as blood. The morning was hot and muggy, the sunlight filtered through a haze. Concrete and steel reflected the heat. In Old Newyork, no trees or grass provided relief. Because he was ill, the old man half wondered if indeed he had begun to sweat blood. He was afraid to wipe his forehead to find out.

Passersby noticed nothing out of the ordinary about him. He was just another sad-faced old man walking the streets. He was thin and stooped, his hair cropped short and gray. Not even the long coat he wore in the heat was unusual. Many moved through Old Newyork with everything they owned. After all, it was easier to wear a coat than carry it.

A closer observer, however, would have seen a certain peace in the man's face. His wrinkles were not set in anger. His eyes were clear. Not many in the slums at his age showed these small indications of hope.

One thing about this man—impossible to see—would have astounded the passersby. Before stepping onto a ferry the day before to cross the river to Old Newyork, Benjamin had been among the richest men in the world. He had given up everything—name, fortune, freedom—just to reach this street corner in the slums.

The old man did not move for several moments. He paused to draw a breath of courage, and looked around with a mixture of sadness and satisfaction. This street corner would suit him now, as it had many years before.

Long ago this area had been a park. A magnificent statue had guarded the entrance to lawn and trees and ponds with fountains. That was before the great Water Wars. Before Technocrats and the World United government. When people still drove gasoline-powered vehicles. When the city was proud and free, not a bombed out island. Not a giant prison where gangs reigned supreme.

Most of the people now passing by had never seen the park of those earlier times. The heavy, tall statue had long since been pulled down for the value of its bronze. All that remained was its high, wide concrete base, stripped, too, of its bronze plaque.

The park itself was now filled with leaning shacks and honeycombed with twisting, littered paths. The fountains had been drained by people desperate for any kind of water. Skyscrapers behind the park cast shadows on the shacks, like mountains overshadowing a village.

Down the street, a waterman sold flasks of water at merciless prices. Bodyguards armed with machine guns protected him. Between the waterman and the old man, vendors of clothes, food, and cigarettes lined the streets, drawing people from their shacks and hiding holes.

Many, many years before, on this same street corner, Benjamin had climbed onto the pedestal of the broken statue before him. He had spoken to the hundreds of people who were scurrying past. Back then his reasons for being here were much different. He had returned today to make up for what had happened because of that first speech.

He drew another deep breath, remembering across the years. He had felt this excitement, hope, and fear then as he had prepared to address the crowd of an earlier generation. It was not easy to speak to a large group of strangers, to gather them together and beg them to listen. Some would laugh. Some would call out insults. And in these slums one could not ask for protection. Not from anyone. Not against anyone.

The excitement, fear, and hope rolled through his belly like kittens tumbling over a ball of yarn. The roof of his mouth, dry from nervousness, tasted of copper. For a long doubting moment, he considered turning away from the street corner and fading back among the street vendors.

Why was he here? What good would it do? How could he hope to make a difference? Thousands and thousands of slum people were spread over dozens and dozens of square miles of street canyons.

He closed his eyes for a moment of prayer.

Prayer calmed him, gave him strength. Not for the first time the old man marveled at the joy and love from the Creator of the universe.

Why was he here? In his mind he saw the mother and father and children he had rescued from the work gangs only hours earlier. They and all the other families like them were his reason for coming here.

What good could he do? None, not by himself. He could only trust the power of a message that had given hope to people throughout the centuries. He could only trust the power of the One behind that message.

How could he hope to make a difference? By planting seeds in soil barren of any hope at all.

"One final breath to calm my nerves," Benjamin Rufus told himself. One final breath of courage. He took in a lungful of air. And coughed. His lungs rattled with pain. With a wry grin, he told himself he deserved the pain for trying to delay his task.

Benjamin moved to the base of the statue. With great effort, he climbed onto the base. For several moments, he swayed on his feet. He closed his eyes and waited for some energy to return.

A few people stared briefly upward at him then ducked their heads and walked by. What was one more madman among them?

When he felt ready, Benjamin reached inside his coat. Twenty-four hours earlier, he had been one of the most powerful men on Mainside. It had been no problem to buy the small electronic device he now pulled from his pocket. It was shaped much like a flip-phone. He slipped its looped cord over his neck, and the device dangled against his chest.

The old man flicked a small switch. Instantly, the microphone at the top of the device was ready to broadcast his words loudly and clearly above the din of the people on the street below.

"People of Old Newyork," Benjamin said. He spoke in a normal voice, knowing his lungs would not permit him any more force. "Listen."

The shock of broadcast words cut through the crowds. Through the shacks behind him. People stared with wonder. Many of them had never heard a voice amplified through speakers. How could this man's words ring through the air like thunder?

Instantly, everyone grew silent.

"Gather close," he urged. "Listen."

Slowly, they began to shuffle toward him.

Benjamin noted that one of the waterman's body-guards sprinted down the street, away from the statue base.

He'd gone to send a message to one of the ganglords. Benjamin knew he had five minutes, maybe ten at the most.

"We all know that there is nothing here of greater value than water," Benjamin said. "Let me tell you about the One who will give you water, so that you will never thirst again."

The crowd muttered excitedly.

"Yes," Benjamin said clearly and slowly. "There is a place waiting for all of you, a place without hunger or fear or thirst. Your greatest hope is because of a man who died on a cross for you. A man from God and of God. A man who rose from the dead."

"No man rises from death!" someone shouted. The crowd hummed with an excited babble of interest and jeers.

"No man born of man," Benjamin Rufus answered calmly. "Let me tell you how this man was different."

As he continued to speak, the old man watched and waited for those who would arrive with spears and crossbows to try to silence him.

CHAPTER 1

MAINSIDE—TWENTY YEARS LATER (A.D. 2096). A luxury high-rise building stood near the Hudson River. From its balconies, it was possible to see the distant slums of Old Newyork on the other side of the river.

Inside the building lay one person who had recently been delivered from Old Newyork. Except he was unaware of his freedom. He was on the tenth floor of the building, on a padded cot with wheels. Plastic tubes connected him to a life-support machine. Other lines were taped to his shaved head and ran to a nitrogen-cooled computer. Two nurses watched his heartbeat and other vital signs with great care. They had instructions to call a team of doctors and comtechs at the slightest sign of trouble.

Down the hall, in a much larger room, the twelve members of the Committee had just gathered around a conference table. A giant vidscreen filled one wall of the room. At the moment no images were on the flat, dull gray screen.

"Cambridge," one of the men said to the Committee leader, "I understand that Mok has moved into stage three."

Cambridge hid a smile of satisfaction. They had all been against the choice of Mok as a candidate.

This was the first time one of them had called him Mok instead of the Welfaro. It was an encouraging sign.

"Stage three," Cambridge confirmed. With hair nearly white, he was tall and thin, and had a face almost hawklike with intensity. As usual, he wore jeans and a casual shirt. "Mok has passed through the pharaoh's tomb and the Holy Land castle. He survived both tests. I expect no problems at all with stage three."

The questioner pointed to the blank vidscreen. "If he is already in stage three, why aren't we able to watch him on the monitor as before?"

Around the room, others nodded and looked at Cambridge expectantly.

Cambridge surveyed them, unbothered by the question.

Some of the Committee members wore business suits. Others had donned the latest fashions in physical training gear, although none of them actually went to the workout centers. They were all in their forties and fifties. These were successful, common-sense men who did not need to wear the black silk togas of Technocrats to boost their egos.

"You all know the situation," Cambridge said to the whole group. "Mok's body is here, but his brain is wired to a cyberspace sequence. He is in a virtual reality stage where the characters and situations have been set up to respond to his decisions. Just as if the experiences were real."

"Yes, yes," the impatient questioner said, still pointing at the screen. "But why can't we see—"

"He is on a ship on the ocean, not a stationary stage like the Egyptian prison or the castle. Unlike the other cyberspace tests, this one is straining our computer to within gigabytes of crashing."

Cambridge checked his timepiece and made some rapid calculations. "In fact, as we speak, Mok is witnessing a pirate raid. It takes many gigabytes of RAM to coordinate the actions of dozens of men, fighting and screaming. Soon, a hurricane will hit. The motion of the ship, the roll of the waves, the creaking masts and pelting rain must all be detail perfect. In short, during this cybersegment, the computer simply can't run the program and still give us a real-time video transmission."

"Later?" another Committee member asked.

"Yes, we can review it later, when there is less memory strain on the computer," Cambridge said. "But remember that our civilized minds will face great shock. Gentlemen, we are talking about an eighteenth-century pirate raid. These men fight with swords, daggers, axes, and short-range pistols. It's savage and cruel beyond our imaginations."

"Savage and cruel!" came the cry from someone near the back. "Followed by a hurricane! What are you putting him through?"

Cambridge allowed a hint of an ironic smile to cross his thin face. "Have some of you actually begun to hope that our final candidate might succeed?"

"Hope is precious," the first speaker said. "Let us at least know that he will have a guide aboard the ship, as he had in previous sequences."

"The presence of a guide would defeat the purpose of this part of the journey," Cambridge said. "And he is on a two-masted schooner, a real pirate ship of that time period."

"Meaning?" someone asked.

"Pace off twenty-four steps," Cambridge said. "That is the entire length of a pirate ship of that era. An open deck twenty-four paces long. And below? Three small cabins forward. One aft. Sleeping hammocks between. With a crew of twenty-five in those cramped quarters, there is no room for a stranger. Not if the cyberspace around Mok is to be believable."

Cambridge regarded the glum faces of the Committee. "All is not lost. I've previously reported of his search for the Galilee Man, as Mok calls Jesus of Nazareth."

They waited.

"We have placed a cross around his neck to remind him of the man of Galilee. And is not Christ, himself, the best guide for any man?"

CYBERSPACE—THE PIRATE SHIP. In the bright sunshine on the deck of the pirate ship, Mok froze as a large man suddenly stepped in front of him.

"And where might you be going?" It was a snarled demand, the tone backed by the gleaming curve of a cutlass. Had Mok taken another step forward, the tip of the sword would have entered his navel.

"Below," Mok answered, refusing to show his fear.

Mok's hidden fear was well-founded. This man, Barbarossa, was the ship's master in charge of all provisions. Mok was carrying some of those provisions—without Barbarossa's permission. This was considered a crime on board a pirate ship.

Mok also knew Barbarossa was a man who enjoyed violence. Mok's dreams, in fact, were haunted by memories of what Barbarossa had done during a raid on a Spanish galleon. That had been before the terrors of the hurricane.

Barbarossa had led the swarming pirates across a rope ladder onto the galleon's deck. Barbarossa had roared with laughter as pistols, cutlasses, and cannon balls cut down the Spanish crew. At the end of the raid, Barbarossa's clothes had been soaked with blood. Others' blood.

Now Mok was face-to-face with this man. By himself. Unarmed.

"Below?" Barbarossa repeated, blinking with suspicion. "You are going below?"

Barbarossa was a brute. His great sloping shoulders bunched at the base of his skull. His nose, once torn and burned by the explosion of gunpowder, had healed into the waxy shine of a molten candle. This was a man who had once lifted two of his own crew mates by their collars—one in each hand—and banged their heads together with such force that both became simpletons. All they had done was make the mistake of laughing when a barmaid spilled beer on Barbarossa.

"Yes, I am going below," Mok said evenly. He had no choice but to answer this man's questions. Mok knew too well there was no place aboard the ship to run or hide. They had not seen land for five days. All that surrounded them was the blue of water and sky, melted together at the horizon. During his first day aboard, the sight of such vast emptiness had frightened Mok. Now, he welcomed the landless sight as the lesser of far worse evils he had recently witnessed. Vast emptiness was much better than a raid. And much better than the two-day storm that had followed almost immediately, a storm that had darkened the morning sky to night. The ship had pitched to the tops of waves as high as the masts and dropped beside the swells to dizzying depths. All the time the hurricane had lashed the air with rain as hard as the shot used in the pistols.

"You carry water," Barbarossa grunted. "And bolts of cloth. For what purpose?"

Other pirates gathered to listen. They could hear a new storm brewing. Much better that Barbarossa's foul temper be directed at someone else—it kept his attention off them. And, in the long days of idleness between raids, it gave them entertainment.

"The water is for the captured men." Mok saw no point in lying, although he could predict Barbarossa's reaction. "Without water, they will die. They also have wounds that need binding."

"The slaves!" Barbarossa roared, to no one's surprise. "Fresh water for the slaves! You steal from us to give to them?"

The other pirates began to mutter. Of any offense a man could commit aboard ship, stealing provisions was the gravest.

"I have Captain Falconer's full permission," Mok said. In the dank dark air below deck, chained to the beam of one of the masts, were five men, the only survivors of the now sunken Spanish galleon. Mok could not speak their language, but he did not need words to understand the agony of these men.

"I am the ship's master!" Barbarossa thundered. "I oversee the provisions. You ask me for water. Not the captain."

"Would you have granted my request?" Mok knew the conversation was becoming more dangerous, but he saw no way to leave it.

"No. I would not. Let the slaves suffer."

Mok decided against the obvious reply. It would be stupid to ask Barbarossa's permission. "The captured men need water. Dead slaves are of no value."

"Neither is a crew member who does not pull his weight." With swiftness unbelievable for such a large man, Barbarossa kicked sideways, hammering Mok at the knees. Mok fell backward. His bowl of water crashed onto the deck beside him. Before Mok could spin or roll, Barbarossa stepped on his chest. Barbarossa pressed the point of his cutlass into the soft hollow of Mok's throat.

CHAPTER 3

BARBAROSSA GRINNED, showing black teeth.

"A crew mate who does not fight has even less value than a dead slave," he told Mok. "For a dead slave will never turn on you in battle."

Without taking the pressure off Mok's throat, Barbarossa looked to his audience of pirates. "Did any of you witness this mate raising a sword or firing a pistol against the Spaniards?"

Save for the creaking of the ship, the flapping of its sails, and the slap of water against the hull, silence was the reply.

"No," Barbarossa said with triumph. "No one saw you join in our fight."

Barbarossa smiled with angry pleasure. "Only the storm spared you earlier. But now I have the leisure to deal with you as you deserve."

The sword pressed against Mok's flesh. He understood in that moment that Barbarossa had been waiting for any excuse to fight him. Mok dared not try to defend himself.

"Yet, you may redeem yourself and keep your life," Barbarossa's voice shifted to a rumble of amusement, "if you prove yourself as one of us."

The other pirates caught the shift in Barbarossa's mood.

"A sporting event?" one asked. "He fights you?"

A fight meant gambling. While they expected Mok to lose, they could wager on how long he stood, if he lived or died, if he lost any limbs, if he was man enough to not beg for mercy. . . .

"Not a fight against me," Barbarossa said. "Against one of the slaves he seeks to help."

Barbarossa stepped away from Mok. "On your feet," he commanded.

Mok stood, resisting the urge to rub his throat.

Barbarossa reversed his cutlass and offered Mok the handle. Mok took it, confused.

"We will bring a slave on deck," Barbarossa said to the other pirates. "He has this sword. The slave will be unarmed."

To Mok, Barbarossa said, "This will be your baptism in blood. Kill, and you survive as one of us. Refuse, and you die in the slave's place."

Mok held the razor-edged cutlass. It would be a simple matter to slash forward and attack Barbarossa. Yet something in the way Barbarossa stood showed he was not only ready but also hoping for Mok to attack him.

Mok dropped the sword.

"No," Mok said. "I will not slaughter any man."

Barbarossa licked his lips. "As I thought. It is the cross around your neck."

Despite the seriousness of the situation, Mok nearly laughed at Barbarossa's words. Yes, Mok wore a cross. But he had no idea how it had gotten there.

The cross around Mok's neck was only the latest of a series of events he could not understand.

Once—it seemed like a couple of lifetimes earlier—he had lived in the slums of Old Newyork. His last memory of Old Newyork was the blue arc of the 'tric shooter that had knocked him unconscious. When he woke, he found himself in a land of sand and pyramids, accused of theft by the pharaoh's daughter. He had survived an execution order, then ended up in a castle under siege. He'd managed to save himself and others there from certain death, and at the final moment of escape, had been drugged. When he came to, he was on this ship. With a strange cross of silver on a fine chain around his neck.

Mok could make no sense of any of it. And least of all, the cross.

"What does the cross have to do with it?" Mok said. He had no understanding of the significance of the silver symbol, let alone any guess as to how or why it had gotten around his neck. He simply knew that he would not kill another man, and that he had dropped the sword without needing to pause to think why.

"There are twenty of us against one of you," Barbarossa taunted. He waved his hands to take in the entire crew. "Will your Jesus save you now?"

11

JESUS, THE GALILEE MAN. Again, mention of the Galilee Man. Mok's skin tingled at the name of this man who seemed to follow him everywhere. Was this Jesus real or legend? And why did the name of this Galilee Man appear in every new place?

Mok kept his questions to himself.

The pirates began crowding toward him.

"The plank," one grinned. "Have him walk the plank."

Mok grabbed the sword from the deck and backed away, aware of how useless the sword was against such a mob.

"Flog him first," another said. "Then have him walk the plank. Let his blood draw sharks."

"Yes! Yes! Bring out the sharks! Drowning is nothing compared to sharks!"

"No, strap him to the mouth of the cannon and shoot!"

Mok felt the backs of his legs bump against the rail of the deck. Behind him were the swells of the depths of the ocean. In front was a mob of men growing more unruly and cruel.

The pirates pressed closer, laughing at Mok's efforts to flail the cutlass and keep them away.

"Stop!" A loud voice commanded.

The laughter and taunts stopped as if sliced by the cutlass in Mok's hand.

"No man dies except by the captain's order."

The pirates parted, giving Mok a clear view of the approaching captain.

Captain Falconer was of medium height and muscular. His reddish-blond beard was neatly trimmed. Normally, he seemed the picture of a country gentleman—an illusion compared to the savage way he attacked and fought enemies. But now his face was haggard, the skin gray as if he were seasick.

"What is happening here?" Captain Falconer asked with quiet authority.

Barbarossa explained. He kept his head raised, staring at the captain with defiance.

"I make those judgments," the captain said. "Not you."

"The same judgment that sent him below with water for the slaves?" Barbarossa asked with a sneer.

"This is my ship, Barbarossa. Speak another word, and you border on mutiny."

Except for the creaking deck and slap of waves against the hull, the ship was silent. The pirates had lost all traces of humor and were straining with tension. If Barbarossa challenged the captain, Falconer would have no choice but to fight a duel. For if he did not take the challenge, Falconer risked losing the ship to Barbarossa.

Barbarossa finally chose to back down. He dropped his eyes and stared at the deck. Mok stored that knowledge and shivered with fear. *Barbarossa, the brute, afraid of Falconer. What kind of man, then, was Falconer?*

The captain turned his attention to Mok. "Barbarossa is right. It is a grave matter that you refused to fight during the raid. Now that the hurricane has ended, it indeed is time I dealt with you. Follow me to my cabin."

CHAPTER 5

MAINSIDE—A.D. 2096. It was just past midnight. Five hours had passed since the Committee members had left the luxury high-rise to return to their homes and estates.

At one of those homes, one Committee member had gone to sleep on his couch wearing a wrist pager. He wasn't surprised when the vibration buzz woke him. Not that he slept well anyway. Traitors rarely do.

He groaned and sat up, rubbing his eyes. This was why he had chosen the couch instead of his bedroom. He did not want anyone in his family disturbed when he answered the page.

He walked quickly from the living room to an office down the hallway. He shut the door behind him and snapped on the light. Although he had expected this call, the Committee member still checked the number on the pager. It confirmed his guess.

He sat at his desk before the vidphone. He dialed a number. Only four people in the entire world knew this number and who it reached. Three were presidents of the biggest country blocs of the World United government. The Committee member was the fourth. At the moment, he took no pleasure in this distinction.

"That took you two minutes," a voice snapped. An image of the president of the World United filled the screen.

"I am sorry, your Worldship," the Committee member answered, keeping his expression neutral. It had only taken him thirty seconds, but no one ever disagreed with the man who headed the World United government. He was the most powerful person among the billions who had survived the Water Wars.

"So tell me some good news," demanded the president. "Tell me that the final candidate is dead."

There was a slight echo to the voice, a delay in transmission. The time gap was the result of scrambling the voice signal between two transmitter satellites. It was impossible for anyone to listen to their conversation with electronic eavesdropping.

"As far as I know, Mok is still alive," the Committee member said. He spoke slowly so the scrambling device could keep pace with his voice.

"What!" Rage filled the president's face. He was a bulky man, with white hair and pale skin flushed pinker than usual in his anger. He wore his customary black silk toga, which signified a high-status Technocrat.

"As we speak," the Committee member said, dreading his message, "he is asleep."

"We cybered an assassin on board that ship! Why hasn't he killed the candidate?"

"Your Worldship, it isn't that simple. The computer program has been set up to cover thousands of variations, all depending on what decisions the candidate makes in cyberspace."

"Listen," the president snarled. "You told me that when a person dies in cyberspace, his brain circuits are sent into shock, which kills him in real time. What's it going to take for our cyberassassin to step up to the candidate and run him through with a sword?"

"Reality, your Worldship. Although we were able to cyber in our killer, he must follow the boundaries of the program. He, too, can only do what the situation dictates. The assassin almost had him, but the captain of the ship stepped between them."

"Why?"

"It was part of the program." The Committee member guarded his expression and suppressed his sigh. "When Mok made his decision not to kill the slave in order to save himself, it was programmed for the pirate captain to appear. Over the next several hours of cybertime—which corresponds with our real time—Mok will sleep. The captain wants him to rest."

"Get to the point," His Worldship snapped. "I want simple answers."

"This stage was not really designed as a test for the candidate. After passing through the first two stages, the Committee agreed it was safe to assume he would not kill a slave on the ship. The pirate captain's role in stage three is to prepare Mok for the fourth stage."

This was why the Committee member had advised that the cyberkiller be sent in after Mok. If he was expecting praise, however, he was disappointed.

"I don't like this," his Worldship said. "Cambridge is a smart man. What exactly do you mean by *prepare?*"

"During the remainder of Mok's time aboard the pirate ship, his only task is to give witness," the Committee member answered. "Cambridge believes that in teaching something, you learn the subject well yourself. It is the same with the act of testifying belief. The teacher gains as much as the student. Cambridge wants Mok's fledging faith to be strengthened. Not tested."

There was silence from his Worldship. Unhappy silence. When he finally spoke again to the Committee member, his voice was ice.

"We have a candidate here who was the first among many to choose justice in ancient Egypt over the opportunity to escape. During the siege in the Holy Lands, he stood for Christ, even though it meant certain death. And here, aboard the pirate ship, Mok has refused to kill a slave to save his own life. And you are telling me his faith needs strengthening?"

"Your Worldship, I—"

"Enough. I need not remind you of how important it is that Cambridge be stopped. I just want one thing: this final candidate destroyed. When do you expect this to happen?"

"Sometime in the morning, your Worldship. No one on the Committee knows yet that we have cybered in a killer. He is free to roam the ship and will wait for the first chance to strike."

"Do not fail," his Worldship said.

CHAPTER 6

CYBERSPACE—THE PIRATE'S SHIP. Mok rose from a bunk against the wall and stretched. Across from him in the cramped captain's quarters, the pirate Falconer sat on a stool and watched him without expression.

Falconer held open his hand. A small cross dropped from it, then dangled in the air. The chain of the cross was intertwined in the man's fingers.

Mok's hands automatically reached up to his neck.

"Yes," Falconer said. "Your cross. I took it from you while you slept."

Falconer handed him back the cross.

"Although Barbarossa has called for your blood," Falconer said, "I have protected you. I gave you food and drink to sustain you, and permitted you a night to rest. Now is time for payment. Answer me these questions. Where are you from? And why do you wear the cross?"

Mok hesitated. Indeed, these were the same questions he had been asking himself. He wondered if even the street canyons of Old Newyork and the Water Wars of his childhood were real. So much had happened to him. First the land of limitless sand. Then the castle. Now he was aboard a pirate ship with a cross in his possession and no knowledge of how he had originally come by it. If only that had been all. But there had also been a troublesome yet helpful dwarf. And a beautiful woman of great mystery.

Falconer mistook Mok's hesitation for reluctance. He lifted his sleeve and pulled out a shining dagger.

"Speak," the pirate captain said. "Or I will remove your tongue so that you may never speak again."

Mok gathered his thoughts. How much could he tell the pirate and still survive?

Falconer sighed and stabbed the dagger into the small table beside him.

"Ignore my threats," Falconer said. "My mind is whirling with confusion. Two days ago, before the great storm, I would have cut your throat and laughed as the ship's cats lapped your blood. Today I am burdened with a promise, and a soul that longs to soar."

Falconer stared at the cross dangling from the chain he had returned to Mok. "During the storm, I feared for my life. For the first time ever, I realized I was as mortal as any other man. Me, a man who cannot be bested with a sword. Me, a man who has sent dozens to their graves. I, too, will die."

Falconer sighed again. Mok sensed it was no time to interrupt.

"So in the fury of the storm," Falconer continued, "as the rain lashed at this ship, as the waves tossed us like a cork, I cried out to God. I swore he could have my soul if he kept us safe."

Falconer smiled sadly. "Even for a pirate like me, an oath made is an oath kept. If I have a soul—and surely I must, if during my greatest fear an instinct told me to call upon the God of the universe—what must I do to give it to him?"

"YOU ARE ASKING me all of this?" Mok said. "Am I to answer these questions?"

"You wear the cross of Christ. Aboard a ship of cutthroats, no less. Your conviction must be great. Share it with me."

From the sands to the castle to the pirate ship, legends of the Galilee Man had haunted Mok, teasing him like fragrance upon a wind. For that reason, Mok nearly laughed at Falconer's question. But the earnestness of the pirate was too great, the hunger on the man's face too sorrowful.

"Very well," Mok said, "I will tell you what I know of the Galilee Man."

When Mok was a child, his most valuable possession had been an audiobook. He had listened to the audiobook again and again, trying to understand its meaning, taking comfort from it. It spoke of a man who gathered twelve followers and called them fishers of men. It spoke of a man who described a place called heaven, where the Father waited—but the audiobook had been stolen long ago. When Mok was a young orphan, hiding on the streets like a rat, those words had been beautiful. As he'd grown, he'd begun to wonder if his precious memorized words were only legend.

So which part of the audiobook should he pass on to this pirate? Mok closed his eyes, choosing words he had listened to during nights of terror, huddled alone in the slums.

"I tell you the truth," Mok repeated from memory, "the time is coming and is already here when the dead will hear the voice of the Son of God. And those who hear will have life."

Mok opened his eyes. He saw that Falconer was not smirking but listening intently.

"But he who follows the true way comes into the light," Mok whispered. "Then the light will show that the things he has done were done through God."

"But what does this mean?" Falconer asked.

Mok paused, struggling to answer. And as he searched his own heart for words, a strange peace entered him, like a ray of joy itself. *All things were made through him,* Mok heard in his mind, not sure if it were memories of the audiobook or a whispering voice in his head. *In him there was life. That life was light for the people of the world.*

A God who created the world. Mok suddenly understood as if a curtain had been lifted to show light beyond. A God who loves all people and sent the Galilee Man to speak directly to them.

The power of this unexplained insight took away Mok's breath. He knew what he would say to the pirate! He knew what the pirate needed to hear!

"For God loved the world so much," Mok said. The peace within him grew as he spoke. Where was the warmth of this peace coming from? "That he gave his only Son that whoever believes in Him shall not perish, but have eternal life."

"Can it be that simple?" Falconer asked.

"The Son of God himself told us that," Mok replied.

Before he could say another word a loud knocking rattled the door.

"Falconer!" Barbarossa bawled from outside. "Falconer!"

"I will not be disturbed," Falconer shouted, without opening the door.

The door shuddered, then crashed open.

Falconer whirled to his feet and faced the broken door.

Barbarossa stepped inside. Three more men backed him.

"Your command matters nothing," Barbarossa said. He held a pistol, pointing it at Falconer's chest. "I have declared mutiny."

CHAPTER 8

MAINSIDE—A.D. 2096. "As I advised earlier," Cambridge told the Committee, "those of you with weak stomachs may wish to take a break. There is food and coffee in the waiting room. You may return after the rest of us have reviewed the battle sequence aboard the pirate ship."

No one moved from the chairs set in front of the giant vidscreen.

"Let me understand," a balding man said, when it was clear everyone planned to stay. He toyed with his pen as he spoke. "We are here to review an episode that has already occurred in Mok's world?"

"Correct," a comtech said, answering for Cambridge. "A replay, so to speak. At this point, while Mok's body is at rest in the lab, he believes he is in the captain's quarters of the ship. As we indicated previously, lack of available computer memory makes it impossible to view Mok in his real time. What we are showing has been saved and pulled from the hard drive. It is the best we can do."

"It is this lag time that makes this meeting urgent," Cambridge said. "I want you to see something. Something I saw early this morning when I reviewed the cybersegment."

Cambridge nodded at the technician, who snapped off a light switch and pointed a remote control at the vidscreen.

For the next ten minutes, the only light in the room came from the swirl of color and confusion on the vidscreen. The committee members watched in horrified fascination. Sword fights, gun powder blasts, and pirate savagery sent two of the Committee into the waiting room. Neither, of course, tested their weak stomachs by eating anything.

The remainder of the Committee members were so involved in the action that when Cambridge snapped on the lights without warning, the seated men looked startled. They needed a few moments to adjust to the reality of the carpeted room around them.

"What is it?" one asked.

"Take it thirty seconds back," Cambridge said. His voice was hard. "Zoom on the brute with the deformed face. And freeze there."

In the silence, they heard the slight whir as the storage disk accessed the footage. Then, with clicks on the remote, the comtech brought a closeup onto the screen as requested.

It showed a man in a shirt soaked with the blood of his victims. He had massive sloping shoulders and a sword in each hand. His nose was a stub with the waxy shine of a molten candle. A crazed grin of joy distorted his face.

"This man is our problem," Cambridge said to the Committee. He turned and spoke to the comtech. "You cannot tell me who he is, can you?"

"I . . . I . . ." the technician stuttered.

"As I thought. Run it back ten more seconds. Then isolate the voices near him. You'll hear someone call him 'Barbarossa.' I do not recall that we cybered anyone of his name or description onto the ship."

The technician replayed the previous ten seconds. The segment confirmed Cambridge's observation.

"Well?" Cambridge said.

"You are right," the comtech said. "Had we created such a character, I would remember the name Barbarossa." The technician shuddered. "And the appearance."

"Then," Cambridge said grimly, "we have a problem. Correction. Two problems."

"Problems?" the balding committee member repeated.

"The first problem is grave. There is a monster of a man aboard the pirate ship. One we did not create or place there." Cambridge began to pace. "Barbarossa is a factor beyond our control. Imagine an actor joining a play without the director's consent. That is our situation. Worse, from his actions, this is an actor on a killing spree. And because we cannot watch the cybersequence as it happens, we have no idea what this man has done in the last few hours."

Muttering began from the Committee members.

The balding man raised his voice. "Who would place this Barbarossa into our cyberspace world? Why? And how could our computer security be broken? Our sequence code was supposed to be impossible to crack."

Cambridge answered slowly. "Those questions, my friends, are our second problem. Graver than the first."

The room burst into the noise of heated discussion. For one of the Committee, however, the indignation, anger, and fear of his words were only for show. For him, the cybersegment was going exactly as planned. Even though they had already discovered the killer.

CHAPTER 9

CYBERSPACE. "Show no fear," Captain Falconer said quietly to Mok. "If they sense it, they will attack you like sharks on blood."

The pirate captain and Mok stood together on the upper deck of the ship. Below them, and ten paces away, the pirate crew was gathered in an unruly mob. Mutiny was the greatest crime that could be committed at sea. Half the crew called for the immediate death of the captain. The other half—with the gravity of their intended crime now sinking in after the anger of rebellion—wanted no part of the actual murder.

The shouted arguments below took attention away from the captain and Mok. Their hands were bound behind them with rough rope. Only Barbarossa—too far away to hear the captain speak to Mok—paid them any heed. Barbarossa's full-stare concentration on Mok was chilling.

It's as if he hates me, Mok thought. *Yet I have done nothing to harm the man. Is it the cross I wear?*

"Listen to them," the captain said, "some are calling for us to be marooned."

"Marooned?" Mok asked. His throat was dry with fear. His world had become a whirlwind.

From near execution in the sands of Egypt to a castle siege in the Holy Lands, it seemed his life was always in danger. Looking down upon swords and angry men was far closer to death than he had yet come.

"Marooned. Set adrift in a rowboat with only a few provisions stored on it. Slight as the chance is, we might drift to land before we die. It is a small mercy, but far better than a rope around the neck."

"Hanging?" With the events of a world so different from Old Newyork tumbling around him, Mok wondered if he had truly gone insane. No, he was not crazy. How could he have created these worlds in his head? The burning pressure of the rope on his wrists was all too real. And his pursuit of the truth behind the man called Christ had started with an audiobook in Old Newyork. The audiobook was not imagined either. How could all of this be? *Hanging?*

"Hanging," Captain Falconer said. "From a rope thrown over the main mast. They are afraid that if I live, the day might come when I return. There is a saying among pirates: A dead man gets no revenge."

A faint smile showed behind his reddish-blond beard. "They will soon find out that is wrong. Dead wrong."

"What?" Mok asked, snapping his thoughts back to the violent confusion around him. "A dead captain can take revenge?"

The wolflike gleam returned as Falconer nodded. "Yes. Without me, they will die."

"But how can that be?" Mok asked. "Once you die, you are . . ."

"Dead?" the captain smiled, and Mok noticed the smile reached the pirate's eyes.

"You have heard the Galilee Man tell us there is life beyond, does he not?"

Mok nodded.

"Still," he said, "if they kill me, they too will perish."

CHAPTER 10

"THEY NEED MY navigation log." Falconer stared straight ahead as he continued to speak. "It is the most valuable thing aboard this ship. Notes and journals about dozens of years and thousands of miles of travel at sea. With me dead and without the journal, they will be lost at sea. And they know it. Until now, that fear has allowed me to control this mob."

"I don't understand," Mok said, forcing himself not to look down at Barbarossa and his executioner's glare.

"Part of my power is my ability with my sword," Falconer explained. "But a captain's real strength is in his navigation experience and skills. Few are those who know how to keep the ship safe at sea, to avoid reefs, to find harbors. The only other person on board with this knowledge is Calico, my second-in-command."

Falconer frowned, pointing with his chin. "Him, the one with an eye patch and red silk shirt. Barbarossa must have convinced him to mutiny. Otherwise there would be no one to guide the ship."

Mok frowned too. "If Calico can guide the ship, why then, with you dead—"

"Are they lost?" Falconer's smile turned deadly.

"Calico, like any captain, is helpless without the navigation log. And no one knows the precautions I have taken. The chest that holds my navigation log must be opened in a certain way. Otherwise a flint sparks and sets off a charge of gunpowder. Not only will those in the cabin be instantly killed, but the log will also be destroyed, and a fire started. Few things are more frightening than a fire at sea."

Mok knew of the buckets of sand placed all around the ship, of the great care taken with lanterns and cooking fires. He could fully understand the panic that would arise from a blaze below decks in the captain's quarters.

Falconer drew a breath and stared at the mob of pirates. "If I die, so will they. It's not much of a consolation, is it?"

Mok and Falconer shared a grim silence.

Mok's mind, however, was not at rest.

"If they choose to hang us," Mok said suddenly, "tell them the navigation log will be of no use to them."

"Why?" Falconer snorted. "So they will examine the chest before we are killed? So it will explode while we are alive?"

"Exactly," Mok said, hurrying his words. Barbarossa had begun to walk toward them. "Some of the crew will die, which helps our odds in a fight. A fire in your cabin will send others below deck. Surely in the confusion we can find a way to escape these bonds, to fight, perhaps to escape in the rowboat. A slight chance is better than no chance at all."

Falconer could not answer, for Barbarossa reached them seconds later. His face, sweating in the noon heat, was hideous.

"Tell me," Falconer began, as if he were merely in conversation over ale with a friend, "how did you convince the crew to mutiny?"

"Your sudden weakness," Barbarossa spat. "Kindness to the prisoners. Saving this wretch from my sword. Only the strong rule, and you are no longer strong."

Falconer's next words to Barbarossa surprised Mok.

"The strong grow old and die," Falconer said. "You, with the strength of five men, will one day be weak and feeble. And what then beyond death? There must be something, Barbarossa. Matters of the soul rule far more than the strong. If that is my sudden weakness, it is a strength you cannot comprehend."

Barbarossa laughed. His foul breath hit Mok, even above the other smells of the ship.

"I have the strength of this sword. And the strength of action," Barbarossa said. He lifted his sword. "I will decide your fate while those fools argue. You both die now."

Mok waited. Would Falconer take his advice?

"Then you will die too," Falconer responded with conviction. "I have hidden my navigation log."

Barbarossa's sword wavered. "It is in the chest in your quarters. Calico knows that."

"Can you be certain?" Falconer asked. "If you kill me and do not find the log . . ."

"You lie," said Barbarossa.

"Surely you understand how the ship will then be lost," Falconer continued as if Barbarossa had not spoken. "You can kill us now. But at least our death will be swift. Yours will take place much slower. A ship lost at sea is a terrible thing."

Barbarossa put his sword down. He directed his voice away from them.

"Calico!" Barbarossa shouted. The din of the pirates quieted when Barbarossa called out. "Calico! Come here and escort the captain to his quarters. Have him open his chest and show you the navigation log."

No! Mok nearly shouted out that single word. *Not Falconer!*

CHAPTER 11

MAINSIDE—A.D. 2096. "All of you, gather round," Cambridge snapped. "Witness what we feared most."

The eleven other Committee members left their chairs to stand before the large vidscreen on the far wall of the carpeted room. The screen danced with motion. They saw the deck of a small wooden ship, sails flapping in the wind. Blue ocean and sky beyond. And a mass of shouting men with raised swords.

This world had recently swirled in the mind of a motionless body in another room down the hall. Had they been in that room, they would have heard Mok's heartbeat blips rise in volume and speed to match the corresponding stress of the cybersegment.

"There, in the middle of the pirates, it's that brute!" one of the Committee members stammered in panic. "The one named . . ."

"Barbarossa," Cambridge said flatly. "The one cybered into our computer by an outside source. This is the latest we have been able to review."

They stood mesmerized by the giant man. Among all the figures on the screen, his size and savage ugliness drew attention.

"Listen," another Committee member said. "He is calling the crew to murder the captain!"

"Murder!" the first Committee member yelped. "That was not part of the program! Mok was to be allowed rest and a chance to learn more about Christ! We have no control over a mutiny!"

"That is exactly our problem," Cambridge said, "No control. Not with a virtual reality renegade set loose in our cybersite."

With a remote activator, Cambridge lowered the volume on the vidscreen.

He glanced at his watch. "This was taken a few minutes ago. At this point, the comtechs are on standby to download the action constantly. They are pushing the computer to its limit so we can watch on a two-minute delay pattern."

"You mean Mok could already be dead?"

"No, his body is still alive. But he is in danger," Cambridge said. He paused and looked around the room. "Our options are simple. We leave Mok aboard the ship for the scheduled time. Or flash him to the next cybersite."

Cambridge held up a hand to forestall any questions. "If we leave him aboard the ship, I believe Mok will be killed. Whoever hacked into our cybersite intends the worst. Barbarossa is proof of that. Why else incite mutiny but to create danger for Mok?"

"It is an easy decision then," said one voice. "Flash Mok to the next site ahead of schedule."

"And how long before Barbarossa follows?"

Cambridge asked. "Whoever cracked our encryption code to place that savage aboard the pirate ship also has the power to send Barbarossa after Mok into the next cybersite. You know what Mok faces next. With Barbarossa there, Mok's odds go from grim to impossible."

"The solution then?" someone countered.

"Modify our encrypted security code. Our hacker won't be able to follow. That's the good news."

He surveyed them all. "The bad news? Our comtechs tell me the code is so complex it will take half an hour to change. Real time here is real time in cyberspace. That means Mok must face another half hour aboard the pirate ship before we can safely send him ahead. A half hour with Barbarossa."

"What if Mok jumps overboard? Even with his hands tied, surely he can tread water for half an hour. The ship will sail on without him and—"

Cambridge shook his head. "Remember? His cyberworld is like a stage. Our computer memory is not large enough to make the oceans beyond the ship real. If he steps off the stage—the pirate ship—he will enter a cybervoid. The sensory shock will scramble his brain circuits. If it doesn't kill him, it will turn him into a vegetable."

"Leave him on board for a half hour!" In direct contrast to Cambridge, the first Committee member was an excitable man. He was pointing at the muted vidscreen and the waving swords. "A half hour in a full mutiny? But if he dies there, he'll die here!"

Cambridge nodded. "Yes. The slash of a sword, a rope around his neck, musket balls through his ribs. Any of it will kill Mok in both worlds. Somehow, he must survive the next half hour."

CHAPTER 12

CYBERSPACE. As Calico walked toward them, Mok nearly buckled with the horror of it. To save his own life, Falconer would have to disable the trap and hand over the navigation log. Then they would surely be killed.

Barbarossa pushed Falconer toward the approaching Calico. Falconer stumbled and turned his head to speak to Mok.

"You spoke of the Son of God," he said quietly. "And I believe. No longer do I fear death as I did during the storm."

Did that mean Falconer would sacrifice his own life to give Mok a chance to escape?

Mok couldn't ask the question aloud. Calico spun Falconer around, and they marched away. That left Mok alone with Barbarossa.

"Now," the giant snarled, pulling his sword loose, "you wretched Welfaro orphan, I will finish with you what I began."

"No!" Mok said, with such force that Barbarossa paused. *Wretched Welfaro orphan?* Mok thought. Here on a pirate ship, how could this brute know of Old Newyork? How could he know Mok was an orphan?

"No? You are bound. I have the sword." Barbarossa unsheathed the sword completely. Its hilt was dull brown with dried blood.

"You called me a Welfaro. I must know why." Again, Mok spoke with such intensity that Barbarossa paused.

"Don't play games with me," the giant snarled. "Surely you know by now I have been sent for you."

"Sent? Who sent you? Why?" *This brute must know what's been happening to me,* Mok realized.

"What does it matter to you?" Barbarossa said. "As soon as your head leaves your body, you will no longer exist. Here or there."

Here? Or there? Mok wanted to beg for answers. It seemed he wanted that knowledge more than he wanted life. Yet the sword was raised. The fire in Barbarossa's eyes would not be quenched with mere words. Mok would now receive neither life nor answers.

He refused to beg.

Barbarossa laughed again. A look of insanity filled his eyes.

Then, incredibly, an explosion rocked the ship. Falconer! He had made the sacrifice. Knowing of the trap, he had decided to open the chest in such a way that the gunpowder exploded.

Barbarossa grunted in puzzlement and looked behind him.

Now! Mok told himself. Later, he could mourn for Falconer.

Sword still raised, Barbarossa stared back at the

black smoke that bloomed from the lower decks. Mok dove past him and sprinted down the steps.

There were shouts and confusion.

Mok's first thoughts were to hide below. All he needed was five minutes alone to loosen the ropes around his wrists. Then he could fight, or perhaps get to the rowboat and drop it into the water. Better the open sea than Barbarossa's sword.

Mok reached the lower quarters seconds later. He did not know if Barbarossa pursued him.

Screams filled his ears.

The prisoners! They were trapped.

For a moment, Mok hesitated. If he helped them, he might not escape.

The screams grew louder.

Hadn't Falconer given his life to save others?

Mok turned toward the screams. He could not let them burn without trying to save them.

MOK DODGED pirates running in all directions. Although he knew time was passing quickly, his next moves were blurs of concentration in the confusion of smoke and flames and running bodies.

Mok found the armory. He secured the handle of a sword between his feet to hold it upright and sawed loose his bounds. Then he grabbed the sword and rushed to the prisoners. One by one, he freed them, explaining his plan in loud shouts, hoping they could understand him.

Mok led the freed men to the armory. They grabbed swords and dashed to the open decks.

There, a few pirates fought, but as time passed the fight faded. The pirates had a more urgent problem. The fire.

Finally, Mok and the prisoners reached the rowboat. As Falconer had promised, it held provisions, stored in small casks.

From the side of the ship, Mok looked at the open water below. Freedom. All he had to do was get off the ship, and he would be free.

The prisoners began to loosen the rowboat. Time seemed to crawl by with the pace of a snail. When the boat was ready to be lowered into the water, the prisoners jumped in and called for Mok.

He set one foot in the rowboat. They were waiting for him to push off toward the water below.

Freedom, Mok thought. Whatever problems faced them on the open sea, at least they had escaped death by fire, rope, or sword.

Then a hand grabbed Mok from behind. The other prisoners fell back in fear.

"Thought you could escape?" It was Barbarossa!

The brute held a dagger to Mok's throat. None of the escaped prisoners could make a move to help Mok as he had helped them.

"Now," Barbarossa said, spinning Mok around to face him. "With no ceremony, you die."

In his mind, Mok called upon the Galilee Man of his childhood audiobook. Mok called, telling himself the Galilee Man was not legend, but truth. He prayed that belief in the Galilee Man led to eternal life as the audiobook had promised.

Barbarossa lifted the dagger and began to slash down at Mok's chest.

And Mok's world dissolved in black beyond any shimmer of light.

CHAPTER 14

MAINSIDE—A.D. 2096. When he was young, the Committee member had nightmares of drowning in mud. In his dreams, he would run and run and run, but the deep mud slowed him down until it dragged him below the surface.

Now, as he stepped off the elevator and into the lobby of the high-rise building, he felt the same fear. Other Committee members were engaged in cheerful conversation. But it seemed like he was sinking in the mud.

Twice before, he had stepped off the very same elevator to reach the very same netphone across the lobby. Twice before, he had promised the most powerful person in the world that Mok would not survive the next cybertest. Twice before, he had been wrong.

And for a third time, he had to report failure.

It was like straining and straining to run through the mud. But it sucked him deeper and deeper.

The Committee member barely cared this time if anyone was watching him. They could assume he was checking for e-mail after the long meeting.

He stood in front of the netphone's keyboard and began to type in the private dotcom number for the president of the World United. A president who would be totally outraged to hear that Mok had moved onto the fourth cybertest.

Seconds later, the system prompted him for his e-mail message. The Committee member slowly typed his message:

> **The candidate is now at stage four. It may be days before I can find the new sequence code to send the cyberassassin after him. What are your orders until then?**

The Committee member hit the send button and walked out of the lobby with shoulders slumped.

When he reached his home a half hour later, he ignored his family and went straight to his office. He powered his computer, plugged in his access code, and checked his electronic mailbox. The president of the World United had already replied:

> **Fool. We have already discussed what to do. And you know where and how to do it. Ask yourself. Him? Or you?**

CHAPTER 15

CYBERSPACE—THE WILD WEST. Night thunder woke Mok. Not thunder from lightning, but thunder accompanied by dust. He couldn't see the dust, but he could taste it. The thunder rumbled and rumbled.

He did not understand.

When his eyes adjusted to the darkness, he saw he was halfway up a hill. The far edge of the valley was a line of black against the lighter sky. He also saw the source of the thunder.

Giant animals. Hundreds and hundreds of them passed below, massed in a great long herd.

Mok shook his head wearily. He was too tired and too weak to care anymore. He curled up and went to sleep, lulled by the steady rumbling of the moving beasts.

He slept until the sun was warm upon his face. Without sitting, he opened his eyes and scanned the wide, empty grasslands of the valley. The giant animals were gone.

Mok turned over and dozed. He did not wake until a persistent fly brushed against his face. He waved it away without opening his eyes. It returned.

Finally Mok muttered in anger and sat upright. He froze as he opened his eyes and began to yawn.

It had not been a fly that tickled his face but a feather—attached to the end of a spear. And the owner of the spear, a bronze-skinned warrior wearing only a loin cloth, sat on a horse and stared down at Mok without a smile.

AUTHOR NOTE

Mok's story is actually two stories. One of the stories, of course, is described in this cyberepisode.

There is also a series story linking together all the CyberQuest books—the reason Mok has been sent into cyberspace. That story starts in Pharaoh's Tomb *(#1) and is completed in* Galilee Man *(#6). No matter where you start reading Mok's story, you can easily go back to any book in the series without feeling like you already know too much about how the series story will end.*

This series story takes place about a hundred years in the future. You will see that parts of Mok's world are dark and grim. Yet, in the end, this is a story of hope, the most important hope any of us can have. We, too, live in a world that at times can be dark and grim. During his cyberquest, Mok will see how Jesus Christ and his followers have made a difference over the ages.

Some of you may be reading these books after following Mok's adventures in Breakaway, *a Focus on the Family magazine for teen guys. Those magazine episodes were the inspiration for the* CyberQuest *series, and I would like to thank Michael Ross and Jesse Flores at* Breakaway *for all the fun we had working together. However, this series contains far more than the original stories—once I really started to explore Mok's world, it became obvious to me that there was too much of the story left to be told. So, if you're joining this adventure because of* Breakaway, *I think I can still promise you plenty of surprises.*

Last, thank you for sharing Mok's world with me. You are the ones who truly bring Mok and his friends and enemies to life.

From your friend,

Sigmund Brouwer

The adventure continues!

Join Mok in the untamed Wild West in

QUEST 4

OUTLAW'S GOLD

It seems for the first time Mok has found
peace and rest. He's helping a preacher
who's working with the Pawnees on the wide
open prairies of the 1870's Wild West. But too
soon, Mok discovers that the lure of gold can
destroy nearly any faith . . . and that life
or death among outlaws depends on more
than a fancy six-shooter pistol.